Molly is New

For Alice

First published 2005
Evans Brothers Limited
2A Portman Mansions
Chiltern Street
London W1U 6NR

British Library Cataloguing in Publication Data
Turpin, Nick
        Molly is new. - (Twisters)
        1. Children's stories - Pictorial works
        I. Title
        823.9'2 [J]

ISBN-10: 0237530686
13-digit ISBN (from 1 January 2007) 9780237530686

Printed in China by WKT Company Limited

Series Editor: Nick Turpin
Design: Robert Walster
Production: Jenny Mulvanny
Series Consultant: Gill Matthews

Molly is New

Nick Turpin
and Silvia Raga

Evans

Molly is new…

...new at school!

7

She has new shoes
and a new bag.

8

School is big.

So is the teacher!

13

14

Molly draws.

16

She pours…

17

...and listens...

...and eats lunch.

It's playtime!

Molly falls.

Her knee hurts.

26

The big teacher
makes it better.

She's nice.

But Mum is nicest!

Why not try reading another Twisters book?